Joey and Sam

"A heartwarming storybook about autism, a fami　　　　other's love."

Written by: Ill　　　　　　o, M.D.

Borowitz

Prologue by: Illana Katz
Epilogue by: Edward Ritvo, M.D.*
* Professor of Medicine,
Department of Biobehavioral Sciences,
Division of Child Psychiatry
and Mental Retardation,
U.C.L.A. School of Medicine

**REAL LIFE
STORYBOOKS**

Northridge, California

"Acts of goodness and kindness bestow immortality."

Our special thanks to Emanuel Schear . . .

**Other storybooks to be released in 1993–1994
by REAL LIFE STORYBOOKS include:**

Show Me Where It Hurts
Uncle Jimmy
Sunshine
Sit Down, Steven!
Dexter And The Clock
Jennie's Piano
Pull Yourself Together, James!

Published by

REAL LIFE STORYBOOKS
19430 Business Center Drive
Northridge, California 91324

First Edition
Text Copyright ©1993 Illana Katz and Edward Ritvo, M.D.
Illustrations Copyright ©1993 Franz Borowitz

Library of Congress Cataloging-in-Publication Data

Katz, Illana, 1946–

Joey and Sam: a heartwarming storybook about a family with an autistic child/written by Illana Katz and Edward Ritvo: prologue by Illana Katz: epilogue by Edward Ritvo: illustrations by Franz Borowitz. p.   cm.

SUMMARY: Although it is sometimes hard to have a younger brother like Sam who is autistic, Joey is proud when Sam's special class performs at a school assembly.

ISBN 1-882388-06-2: $9.95

(1. Autism — Fiction. 2. Brothers — Fiction.) I. Ritvo. Edward. 1930– . II. Borowitz, Franz, ill. III. Title.

PZ7.K15744Jo   1993   (Fic) — dc20   92-38812 CIP AC

For Seth . . .

MOTHER TO HER AUTISTIC CHILD

Tell me, my love,
Tell me what you see.
Let me know how you feel,
What you dream about,
What you're thinking.

Look into my face.
I need to see your shiny, smiling eyes lock onto mine,
Your inner soul merge with mine.

Let me hear you speak.
Let me hear your words,
Crystal clear,
Pregnant with meaning.

Allow me to give you the gifts I have to offer.
I gave you life,
But there is so much more we need to share.

Can you question?
Can you seek answers?

What do you think about flowers and rivers, birds and streams?
Smell the flowers.
Look at their colors, their shapes.
Do they have fragrance?

The water, is it cold to the touch?
Do you hear its sounds rippling along the brook?
Can you see your gentle face in its mirror?

The songs of the birds, are they different?
The woodpecker over there,
Can you see him?
Do you hear his sounds?
What of that owl who hoots from a distant tree.
Are you aware?
Run, catch the lovely butterfly lighting upon a nearby flower.

Are you sometimes afraid, sometimes lonely?
Ask me, "Why". Why is such a wonderful word. Why initiates.

Share yourself with me. I promise to listen.
I am here for you, my child. Always.
I will stand beside you. Always.
I promise to love you. Always.

Illana Katz

Joey heard a noise. He woke up. He opened his eyes.
It was very early. The sun was waking up, too.
It is the first day of spring, thought Joey.
Today will be a special day at school.

Joey looked across the room at his brother's bed.

"Sam," said Joey, "Where are you?"

Joey sat up.

Sam was walking around the room.

He was talking, but Joey could not understand him.

He was waving his hands in the air.

He was walking on his toes.

"Hey, Sam, sit down," said Joey.
"It's not time to be out of bed yet.
I want to sleep."

Sam sat down for a minute.

Then he popped up again.

"Mommy," called Joey. "Sam's up."

A minute later Mommy opened the door.

"Did you call me, Joey?" she asked.

"Yes," he answered. "Sam won't sit down.

He is making noise.

I want to sleep. I'm tired."

"Why can't he be like other brothers?" asked Joey.
"Why is he different?"

Mommy thought about Sam a lot.
Sam looked like other children,
but he was different.
Sam had autism.

Mommy smiled and kissed Joey.

"I love you, Joey," she said.

Being six is hard, Joey thought sadly.

It is especially hard when you have

a five-year-old brother like Sam!

Mommy and Sam went downstairs to the kitchen.

"Do you want some milk?" Mommy asked Sam.

"Do you want some milk?" echoed Sam.

"Do you want some?" she asked again.

"Want some," said Sam.

Sam was thirsty. Mommy poured him a big glass of milk.
He wiggled his fingers in front of his face.

Soon Daddy came down to the kitchen.
"What's for breakfast?" he asked.
"How about pancakes?" asked Mommy.
"Everyone loves to eat my pancakes."
"Sam is hungry," Sam said. He walked around
the kitchen tapping his hands on the table.

The smell of pancakes filled the house.
Joey came into the kitchen.
"I smell pancakes. Can I have some, too?" he asked.

"Of course," said Mommy as she set the table.
Everyone sat down. Everyone except Sam.
He walked around and around.

"Sit down, Sam," said his father. "It's time to eat."
Sam did not listen.
"Sit down, Sam," said his mother. She took his hand.

Sam sat down. He did not look at his mother. He did not look at his father. He did not look at his brother Joey.
But he did eat his pancakes.

"Be careful, Sam," said his mother. "The pancakes are hot."
"Mercury is hot and dry," Sam said. "It is a planet.
It is close to the sun."

"Why can't he be like other brothers?" cried Joey.
"Why do I have to have a brother like him?
He can't play games the way I do.
Sometimes he holds his ears or makes funny sounds.
Sometimes he lies down on the floor and kicks his feet.
He spins around and around in the supermarket, too.
People look at Sam. My friends laugh at him.
They don't even want to play here."

"I told my friends that Sam had a problem," continued Joey.
"I told them Sam had autism.
I told them they could not catch it.
It is not like a cold.
I told them that it begins when you are very little.
Maybe you are even born with it."

"My friends just don't understand," said Joey sadly.
"Why can't the doctor fix him, Dad?"
Tears came down Joey's face. He felt sad. He felt angry, too.
"It's not fair," he continued.
"Nobody has a brother like Sam, except me!"

Sam sat down next to Joey. He closed his eyes. He was sad inside. Sam knew he was different. But he could not understand **how** he was different. He did not understand **why** he was different. Sam put his arms around his brother. "Sam loves Joey," said Sam quietly.

At 8 o'clock the schoolbus came.

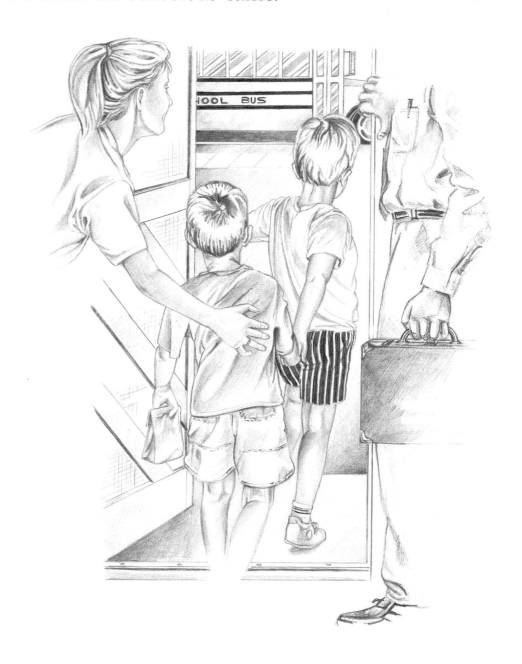

Joey kissed his mother and hugged his father.
He took Sam by the hand and went outside to the bus.

"Good morning, boys," said the bus driver.

Sam looked at the floor.

"Good morning, Mr. Mack," said Joey.

"Please sit down and put on your seatbelts," said Mr. Mack. Off went the bus. In a few minutes it stopped at the school.

Joey walked with his friends to his room.

He was in the first grade.

There were many children in his class.

His teacher, Miss Judy, was always busy.

The children sat quietly. They did their work.

Miss Terry, one of Sam's teachers, took him by the hand.
They walked to the other side of the school.
There were three teachers and six children in his class.
All the children had autism. The room was very noisy.

At ten o'clock Joey went outside to play.

He played catch with his friends.
"I like to play games with all of you," he said. "It's fun!"

Sam went outside, too.

Mr. Reed, a special teacher, came to show Sam how to
throw and catch a ball.
"Catch the ball," he said to Sam. Sam missed the ball.
Mr. Reed threw the ball again.
"Catch the ball, Sam," he said again. Sam reached up.
He caught the ball. "Good for you!" shouted Mr. Reed.
Sam smiled.

It was time to go inside. It was time to work.
Miss Betty, the speech teacher came to
help the children.
Sam's class was very busy.
Soon the lunch bell rang.

Joey and Sam did not eat together. Joey ate with his friends.
Sam ate with his class and his teachers.

"This is a special day," said Miss Terry.

"This afternoon is our Spring Sing. Let's get ready."

All the children sat down in the auditorium.
First, Joey's class sang three songs.
Everyone clapped their hands, even Sam.

Sam's class was next. They stood up. Sam read a poem.
"Wow, Joey! I didn't know your brother could read,"
said Joey's friend Andy.

Then all the children did a special spring dance.
"Sam can dance, too," said Joey's friend Josh.

"Hurrah, Sam!" shouted Joey.

"Hurrah, Sam!" shouted Joey's friends.

Joey walked up to Sam.

"I'm glad you are my brother.

I'm proud of you," he said.

"I love you even if you are different.

I love you even if you never get better.

I love you the way you are!"

We hope **JOEY AND SAM** enables you to help your children be compassionate and understanding when playing with other children who are not developing normally. This is especially important when their playmate, who suffers from a developmental disability, looks normal and may often act normally. That is the reason we chose autism as Sam's developmental disability. Autism has no unique physical characteristics and its symptoms may wax and wane.

For those of our readers who are interested in more information about autism, we offer the following:

- Autism affects approximately one person in twenty-five hundred and is found in all countries around the world. It is more common in males than females. Females with autism are usually more seriously impacted than males. Autism strikes families of all races, religions, and social classes equally.

- There is no exact medical or psychological test for autism. Rather, the unusual way that a child develops leads to the diagnosis.

- The developmental difficulties and symptoms of autism are due to the fact that certain parts of a child's brain either fail to develop, only partially develop, or develop slowly. If the parts of the brain that control intelligence are spared, or are only minimally affected, the person can have normal or above average intelligence. If those same parts fail to develop, or are severely damaged, the person will be unable to pass the usual intelligence tests and will be classified as mentally retarded. At least two-thirds of the autistic people seen in our clinics are seriously affected enough to be classified as mentally retarded.

- The cause of autism is not known. However, we know it is not caused by anything the mother did when pregnant, during the delivery of her child, any special medical disease, nor any medicine the child took as an infant.

- Some families have more than one child with autism. In these families we suspect an inherited predisposition may exist.

- Autistic children live a normal life span and may continue to have symptoms when adults. In the vast majority of autistic people the brain continues to develop new functions throughout the teenage years. Even those people seriously disabled when young may, as adults, live in the community and support themselves with minimal assistance. People who have very mild cases of autism may appear quite normal when adults. These people often marry and frequently have children.

- There is no known medical, psychological or educational treatment that can change the natural course of autism in any given person. However, there are many ways we can help autistic people overcome or minimize their handicap. All autistic people should receive behavior therapy and special education by highly trained specialists familiar with autism.

If you wish further specific information concerning autism please write to:

Edward R. Ritvo, M.D.
in association with Illana Katz
U.C.L.A. Medical School
Neuropsychiatric Institute
760 Westwood Plaza
Los Angeles, CA 90024